Smarty Prince

Written by Sarah Albee

Illustrated by George Ulrich

Clip-clop, clip-clop, clip-clop.

A clever prince was riding through the forest one day when a piece of paper floated through the air and landed in his hands. "Hark!" he said, reining in his trusty steed and studying the paper. It was full of mathematical calculations. "What is this?" he wondered.

The paper seemed to have come from a small window at the top of a very high tower.

"Someone must be imprisoned in that tower," thought the prince. "Perhaps it is a clever princess, and she is trying to calculate how to get down."

He leaped from his horse. "I will have to rescue the fair maiden!" he said. He stared up at the window. "But it will be a challenge to climb this high tower."

Luckily, the prince liked challenges. After scribbling down a few mathematical calculations of his own in a small notebook, he clapped it shut and then rummaged through his horse's saddlebags.

"Aha!" he said, as he took out some plungers. "These are just the tools I need!"

Splonk! Splonk! Splonk! Up, up, up he climbed, carefully placing one plunger at a time as he inched his way to the top of the tower. But halfway up, he hit a patch of slippery moss.

Pfffffffff! Down he slid, landing with a bump at the bottom.

The prince was not the sort of person to give up easily. Once more, he jotted down a few equations in his notebook and then rummaged around in the saddlebags.

"Aha!" he said, and he took out a hammer and nails. Then he gathered some wood planks that were leaning against the base of the tower. The prince began to construct some steps up the side of the tower.

Up, up, up the prince climbed, hammering new footholds as he went. But when he was three-fourths of the way up, his plan fell apart. There were no more planks.

With a heavy sigh, the prince was forced to climb back down, removing his unsuccessful staircase as he went.

Undaunted, the clever prince thought and thought, and then he thought some more. His horse tossed its head and whinnied. This gave the prince another idea!

He pulled a rope out of the saddlebag and tied one end to a rock. Then he flung the rock up, up, up and over the branch of a tall tree. He untied the rock and tied that end of the rope to his horse. The other end he tied around his own waist.

"Steady, now," he said, giving his trusty steed a little pat on the rump. Luckily, it was a very clever horse. It began to walk away from the tree. The rope went taut, and the prince was lifted up, up, up to the high window.

"Uh, hello!" called the prince when he reached the window.

A lovely princess was sitting at a desk, writing on a piece of paper. She looked up to see who was speaking. The prince smiled and bowed, or bowed as best he could while suspended from a rope high above the ground.

"I found your interesting calculations," said the prince, holding up the now-crumpled piece of paper for her to see. "I am a clever prince. Will you help me climb through this window?" he asked.

Although quite surprised, the princess put out her hand and hauled in the dangling prince. He untied the rope and dusted himself off.

"I have come to rescue you, fair princess. And after that," he said, getting down on one knee, "I hope you will marry me."

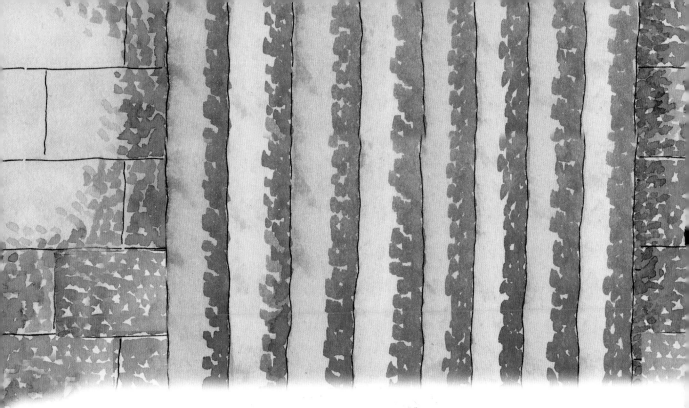

The princess was very puzzled. "How can I possibly marry someone I have only just met? Perhaps we can descend this tower and go to my father's palace. We can get to know each other better over a game of badminton and some mugs of milk."

The prince, who, as you know, liked a challenge, scrambled eagerly to his feet. "Of course," he said with a bow. "First things first." He flipped open his little notebook and, lost in thought, chewed the eraser at the end of his pencil.

"Now what in the world are you doing with that notebook?" inquired the princess.

The prince looked up from his calculations. "I am figuring out the best way to get you down from this high tower, fair princess," he said. "I've almost got it worked out. I welcome a challenge."

The princess gave a tiny cough. "I don't need to be rescued, thanks all the same," she said. "I like it up here. It's where I do my homework. Besides, to get down, all we need to do is . . .

". . . take the elevator."